PANCHO'S PIÑATA

PANCHO'S PIÑATA

Stefan Czernecki and Timothy Rhodes

Illustrations by Stefan Czernecki

Hyperion Books for Children

An enormous cactus, bristling with spines, grew in the center of the village of San Miguel. The cactus was much older than anyone in the village and very likely older than the village itself.

On Christmas Eve everyone in the village dressed up in their finest clothes to join in a procession to reenact Joseph and Mary's long ago search for lodging. Heading this *posada*, as the procession was called, was a little boy dressed as an angel. Behind him, carried on a small platform, were painted clay figures of Mary seated on a burro with Joseph walking beside her.

When the procession finally entered the square, the villagers gathered around a Nativity scene set up beside the old cactus. A little clay figure of the Christ Child was laid in its cradle. Then all the villagers rejoiced with singing and dancing.

Just before midnight the boy who was dressed as an angel began to sing. The happy sounds of his song rose above the old cactus and disappeared into the quiet dark of the night. On this particular Christmas Eve a small star listened to the merriment below. It was so enchanted with the sweetness of the singing that it decided to come closer in order to hear better.

Down it sped out of the sky, faster and faster, toward the village festivities below. Just as it thought it was close enough, the star felt a sharp prick. The little star was impaled on one of the sharp spines that grew near the top of the cactus.

"Help! Help!" cried the little star as it struggled to be free. "Help! Help!" it cried again, but no one could hear it over the sounds of the band playing.

As the church bells chimed midnight, the little star watched as one by one the villagers disappeared into the church. Finally, only one person remained in the square — the little boy who was dressed as an angel. He had a pair of paper wings tied to his back, and he carried a wooden shepherd's staff that had a dove carved at its end. His name was Pancho.

The little star took a deep breath and called out again as loudly as it could, "Help me!"

Pancho heard the faint cry and stopped to listen more carefully.

"Up here!" the star called out. "Up here! Up here!" it said again, until Pancho realized that the cries were coming from the top of the cactus.

"What are you doing up there? Who are you?" Pancho asked as he reached up with his wooden staff. He poked and waved the staff about until his arms hurt, but he could feel nothing. The star's light was now so faint that it was barely visible against the night sky. Just when he was about to give up, Pancho's staff struck the cactus in such a way that the star was knocked free of the sharp spine.

The star burst upward into the dark sky, leaving a trail of shimmering stardust that drifted quietly down to earth. Some of the dust settled on Pancho. As he gazed up at the pale twinkle of light, he felt warm and happy. He had been given a wondrous gift.

The years passed, but his happiness remained with him. Even though Pancho worked very hard and he was poor, he was content with his life. Every night he thanked the little star.

One night, near Christmas, as Pancho lay in his bed watching the star through the window, he had an idea. He pulled himself out of bed and stumbled in the dark to the kitchen cupboard. Behind a sack of corn flour he found the pouch that contained the few coins he had managed to save. "I, too, can give wondrous gifts," he said.

Early the next morning, before the first rooster had crowed, the old man set off for the market. He bought toys and fruits and nuts and candies and glue and cardboard and colored tissue paper and ribbons. He could hardly carry all his purchases home.

In the corner of the kitchen was an old clay pot that Pancho had been saving for a special occasion. He dusted it off and set it on the table.

The old man was excited now. He cut up the cardboard and the tissue paper. Then he made tall cones from the cardboard and glued them to the clay pot. Next he covered each of the cones and the clay pot with the colored paper and tied ribbons to the tips of the cones.

When he finished, the clay pot had been transformed into a colorful star as beautiful as the one in the night sky. He filled his star with all the toys and fruits and nuts and candies and then glued down the lid over the small opening that he had made.

As he marveled at his creation he wondered what to call it. He remembered that the traveling merchant who had sold him the clay pot had told him wonderful tales about it. He couldn't remember the tales, but the name *piñata* came to his mind, so that is what he called his wondrous gift.

Early that Christmas Eve, Pancho took his star to the village square and hung it on a rope that he had suspended across the square. One end of the rope was left hanging to the ground. That evening, as the *posada* entered the square, the villagers were amazed to see the beautiful colored star hanging there. As everyone sang and danced, the old man gathered all the children in a circle beneath his *piñata*.

One at a time, and each in turn, he tied a blindfold around the children's eyes, placed a long wooden stick in their hands, spun them around and around, and told them to try to hit the *piñata* with the stick. Most of the time the children flailed at the air as Pancho pulled on the rope to make the *piñata* dance up and down and back and forth. The children laughed and screeched at their clumsy efforts to play Pancho's game.

Suddenly one of the children struck the *piñata* just right. With a loud cracking sound it broke open and showered its gifts on the children below. There was a great scramble to catch the prizes, and soon pockets were bulging with the treats. The children told Pancho that this was the happiest Christmas they had ever known.

When all the villagers had disappeared into the church for midnight mass, Pancho sat down beside the cactus. The star cast its pale light on the weary old man, and he gazed up at it fondly. "Well, little star," he said, "I think I have passed on the wondrous gift you gave to me so long ago."

The little star gathered up all its energy and shone as brightly as it could to show its approval. As the old man watched, the star grew more brilliant and settled itself directly over the cactus.

"Well, well," muttered Pancho. "You really are the Christmas star."

The tale of Pancho and his *piñata* is so old that no one knows whether or not it is true. Yet to this day, on Christmas Eve, the children of San Miguel gather beside the old cactus in the village square to free gifts from a *piñata*. At midnight, when the church bells ring out, the brilliant Christmas star sends down showers of light. Some say that if you look closely you can see the form of a small angel with paper wings in the center of the light.

About piñatas

The *piñata* has an interesting background. The idea of a vessel containing gifts originated in China and was probably brought to Italy by Marco Polo. In Italy the clay pot was the vessel and was used at parties by rich matrons who filled it with jewels and trinkets for their guests. It was called a *pignatta*.

The idea spread to Spain, where the clay pot, the *olla*, was used to hold the gifts. The practice continued in Mexico, where the *olla* was elaborately decorated with papier-mâché and was called a *piñata*.

The *piñata* continues to be used by Spanish-speaking peoples to celebrate Christmas and birthdays.

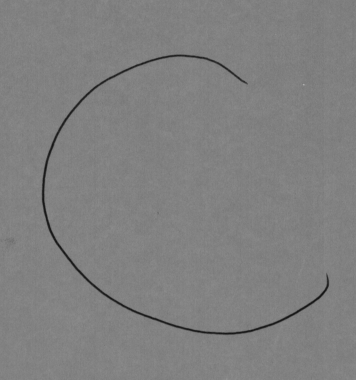